This Topsy and Tim
book belongs to

_____

Topsy and Tim
Meet the Police

By Jean and Gareth Adamson

Illustrations by Belinda Worsley

A catalogue record for this book is available from the British Library

Published by Ladybird Books Ltd
A Penguin Company
Penguin Books Ltd., 80 Strand, London WC2R 0RL, UK
Penguin Books Australia Ltd., 707 Collins Street, Melbourne, Victoria 3008, Australia
Penguin Group (NZ) 67 Apollo Drive, Rosedale, North Shore 0632, New Zealand

004

© Jean and Gareth Adamson MCMXCV
Reissued MMXIV

ISBN: 978-1-40930-883-6
Printed in China

www.topsyandtim.com

One morning Topsy and Tim were in a great
hurry to get to school.
"The police are coming to talk to us today,"
they told Mummy.

When they reached school a police car was already there.
A policeman and a policewoman got out.
"Can anyone tell us where to find Miss Terry?" they asked.
"Why? What's she done?" said Andy Anderson.

Topsy and Tim knew where to find Miss Terry.
"Miss Terry is our teacher," they said.

"Police Constable Webb and Police Constable May have come to tell us all about the work that the police do," said Miss Terry. "Do any of you children know the jobs that the police do?"

"They catch burglars," said Andy Anderson.
"They look after traffic," said Tim.
"They find you when you are lost," said Topsy.
"Yes, we do all those things," said PC Webb,
"and we look after lost things as well as lost children."

"Suppose Tim was walking down the street," said PC Webb, "and he found a purse full of money on the ground. What should he do?"
"Spend it?" said Andy Anderson.
"No," said PC Webb. "That would be very wrong. He should take it to a police station."

"Suppose Topsy was the one who had lost the purse,"
said PC May. "What should she do?"
None of the children knew.
"She should go to the police station and tell them she
had lost her purse," said PC May. "Then the police
would be able to give it back to her."

PC May asked Topsy and Tim to help her
pin up some pictures of the police at work.
One of the pictures showed a police dog.
"Have you got a police dog?" asked Topsy.

"No," said PC May. "Police dogs belong to police dog handlers. The dogs are trained to find things that are lost or hidden. They are very clever."

PC Webb told the children that one of the most important jobs the police do is to come into schools and talk to children about safety.
"Some places are dangerous to play in," he said.

The children helped PC Webb think of some dangerous places.
"Don't play near deep water – you might fall in," said Kerry.
"Don't play by a railway line – a train might hit you," said little Stevie Dunton.
"Don't play on a building site – you could cut yourself on something sharp and rusty," said Louise Lewis.

"Always stay where your mother can keep an eye on you," said PC Webb, "and never ever talk to strangers. If a stranger tries to talk to you in the street or anywhere else, don't let them come near you."

"What is a stranger?" asked Tim.

"A stranger is someone you don't know," said PC Webb. "Most people are good and kind, but there are some people who like to take children away and hurt them. So NEVER get into a stranger's car – even if they know your name and seem nice and friendly."

"If a stranger has tried to talk to you, or asked you to get in his car, tell your mummy or your teacher and they should tell the police," said PC Webb.

PC May helped the children act a play called Stranger-Danger.
Andy Anderson was the bad stranger.
"Will you help me find my lost puppy?" he said to Vinda.
"No!" shouted Vinda, keeping out of his way.

Rai was Vinda's daddy. He took Vinda to the police
station to see PC Topsy and PC Tim.
"My little girl says a stranger frightened her," said Rai.
"Thank you for telling us," said Tim. "We will try and
catch that bad man."

After the play it was time for PC Webb and
PC May to go back to their police station.
The children waved goodbye.

On their way home from school that day Topsy
saw something shiny on the pavement. It was a
very pretty brooch.
"Someone will be sad to have lost such a nice
brooch," said Mummy.

"We must take it to the police station,"
said Tim. "Then the police can give it
back to the person who lost it."

"Hello," said the desk sergeant in the police station.
"Can I help you?"
"Topsy's found a pretty brooch," said Tim.
The desk sergeant took the brooch and wrote about
it in her book.

They went home and were having tea when the phone rang. Dad answered it. It was the police to say that they had found the owner of the lost brooch. "I wonder who it belonged to?" said Mummy.

That night, when Topsy and Tim were getting ready for bed, there was a knock at the door. It was Mrs Higley-Pigley. "Thank you, Topsy and Tim," she said, "for finding my very special brooch and for taking it to the police."

Now turn the page and help
Topsy and Tim solve a puzzle.

Look at this picture of the police arriving at Topsy and Tim's school. Can you work out where each jigsaw piece should go in the big picture?

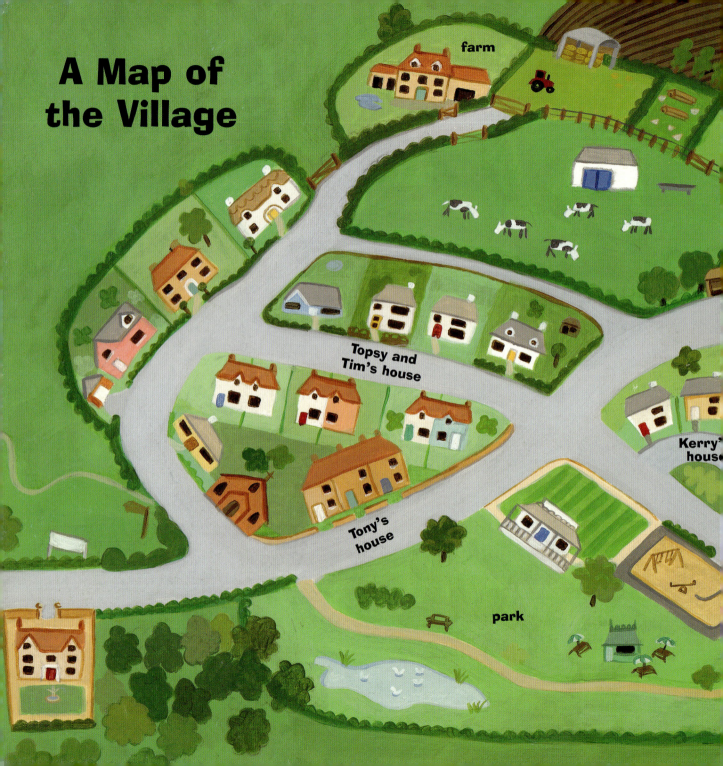

A Map of the Village

farm

Topsy and Tim's house

Tony's house

Kerry's house

park

police station

nursery school

primary school

church

health centre

post office

garage

Have you read all the Topsy and Tim stories?

 Topsy and Tim **Visit London** 9781409309475

 Topsy and Tim **The New Baby** 9781409300564

 Topsy and Tim **Have Itchy Heads** 9781409307204

 Topsy and Tim **Sports Day** 9781409309468

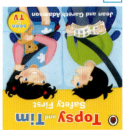 Topsy and Tim **Safety First** 9781409308829

 Topsy and Tim **Play Football** 9781409303350

 Topsy and Tim **Learn to Swim** 9781409300601

 Topsy and Tim **Meet the Firefighters** 9781409307211

 Topsy and Tim **Go to the Zoo** 9781409300847

 Topsy and Tim **Meet the Police** 9781409308836 ✓

 Topsy and Tim **Meet Father Christmas** 9781409311591

 Topsy and Tim **Have a Birthday Party** 9781409300618

 Topsy and Tim **Go to the Dentist** 9781409300588

 Topsy and Tim **Go to the Doctor** 9781409303343

 Topsy and Tim **Start School** 9781409300830

 Topsy and Tim **Go to Hospital** 9781409304234

 Topsy and Tim **Go on a Train** 9781409304241

 Topsy and Tim **Go on an Aeroplane** 9781409300571

 Topsy and Tim **Go Camping** 9781409303336

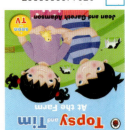 Topsy and Tim **At the Farm** 9781409303367

The Topsy and Tim app is available for iPad, iPhone and iPod touch.

It is also available on Android devices.

 Available on the App Store